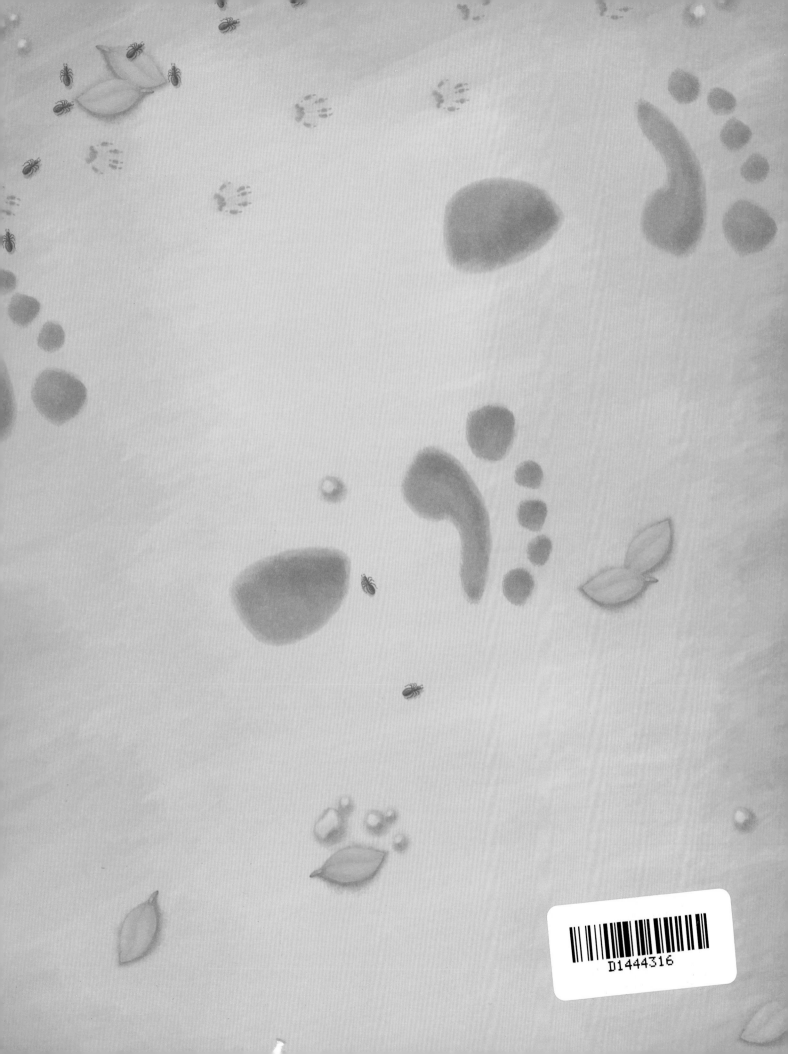

D1444316

MR. BIGGS
in the City

written and illustrated by
Kevin Bloomfield

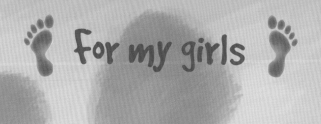

for my girls

©2011 Raven Tree Press

All rights reserved. For information about permission to reproduce selections from this book, write to: Permissions, Raven Tree Press, a Division of Delta Systems Co., Inc., 1400 Miller Parkway, McHenry, IL 60050 www.raventreepress.com

Bloomfield, Kevin.

Mr. Biggs in the City / written and illustrated by Kevin Bloomfield;
—1 ed. — McHenry, IL ; Raven Tree Press, 2011.

p. ; cm.

SUMMARY: Will Mr. Biggs find out that he fits in the city… or is he too big?

English Edition
ISBN 978-1-936299-26-3 hardcover

Bilingual Edition
ISBN 978-1-936299-24-9 hardcover

Audience: pre-K to 3rd grade.
Title available in bilingual English-Spanish or English-only editions.

1. Humorous Stories — Juvenile fiction. 2. Animals — Juvenile fiction.
3. Folklore — Juvenile fiction. I. Illust. Bloomfield, Kevin. II. Title.

Library of Congress Control Number: 2010936672

Printed in Taiwan
10 9 8 7 6 5 4 3 2 1
First Edition

Free activities for this book are available at www.raventreepress.com

PRINTED WITH
SOY INK

Raven Tree Press
A Division of Delta Systems Co., Inc.
www.raventreepress.com

Mr. Biggs is a Sasquatch.
Some call him Bigfoot.

Mr. Biggs lives in a cozy little cave in the middle of the forest.

4

Mr. Biggs loves to climb trees.

When he climbs to the top of the tallest tree, he can see everything in the city.

Mr. Biggs spots so
many interesting things.

6

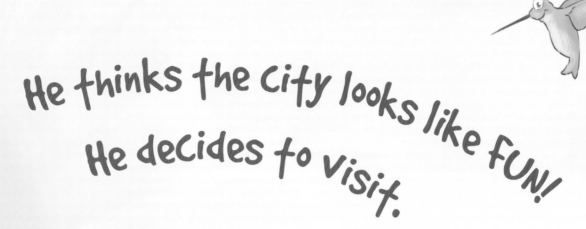

He thinks the City looks like FUN!
He decides to visit.

Mr. Biggs hikes through the forest. He peeks through the bushes at the edge of the city.

There are so many
fun things to do.

Mr. Biggs tries to ride a shiny, red bike.

10

He tries to be a tough policeman, too.

THIS IS NOT FUN.

11

Mr. Biggs tries riding a roller coaster...

and skateboarding.

This is not FUN, either.

Mr. Biggs even tries ballet...

14

and gets a haircut.
This is definitely not fun.

Mr. Biggs tries to play
an electric guitar...

16

then tries to drive a car.
This is no fun at all.

BIGGS

and jogs through the park.
Is this fun?

19

Mr. Biggs stops to see kids having fun.
He wants to have fun, too.

Mr. Biggs sits on the swing.

22

He tries the slide.
This is not fun.

23

Mr. Biggs tries the monkey bars.

He tries the teeter-totter, too.
This is not fun, either.

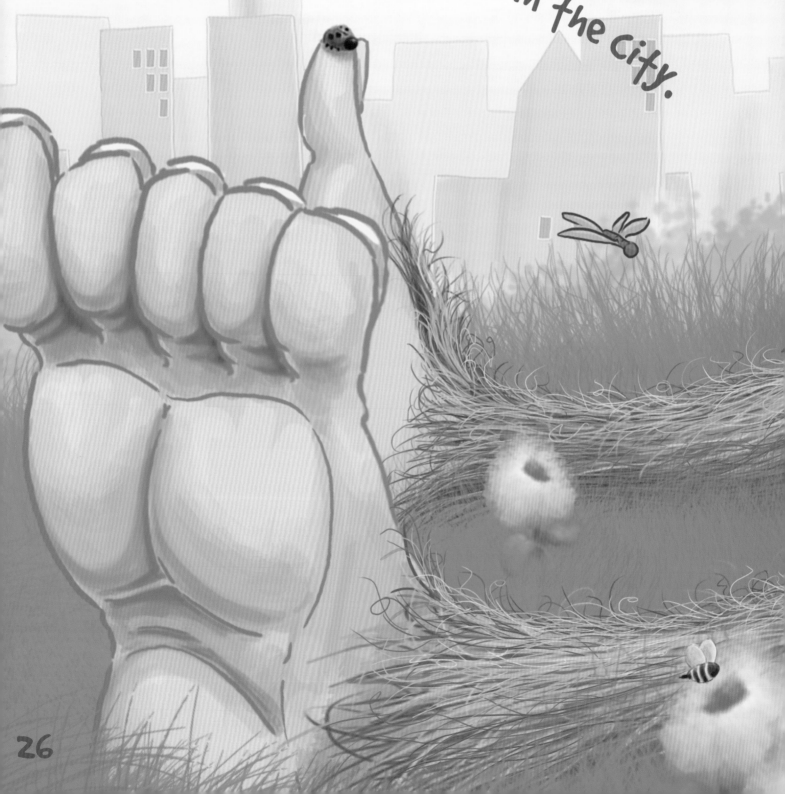

Sadly, Mr. Biggs doesn't think he will ever have fun in the city.

The children see Mr. Biggs and run to him.

They climb on him, play with him, and laugh with him.

Mr. Biggs finally knows how to have fun in the city.

"I ruuv kids!"

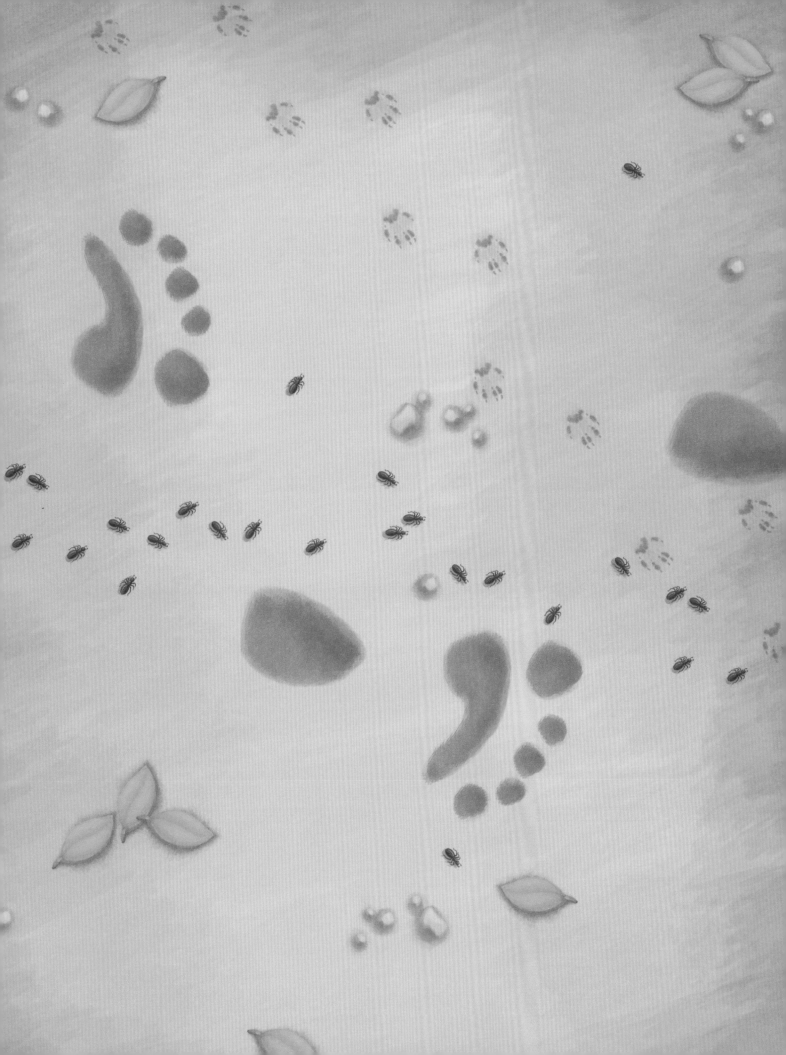